Millie the Mole
and the Unfamiliar Hole

Mary Jane Pearce

Illustrations by Hulya Harber

Bonker Books

www.bonkerbooks.com

Millie the Mole
and the Unfamiliar Hole

Mary Jane Pearce

Illustrations by Hulya Harber

Published by Bonker Books

Bonker Books

www.bonkerbooks.com

ISBN 978-0-9558184-5-5

Printed in the United Kingdom

A catalogue record for this book is available from the British Library

Against her mother's wishes, Millie had burrowed in different directions all day. Exhausted, she eventually fell asleep at the end of a very long tunnel.

After some time, Millie woke up. Alone and cold, the unfamiliar smell of cement and chemicals made her sneeze. Millie scrambled upwards, but was shocked to find that the surface was unbreakable. Digging to her left, Millie eventually came up alongside a shiny new road.

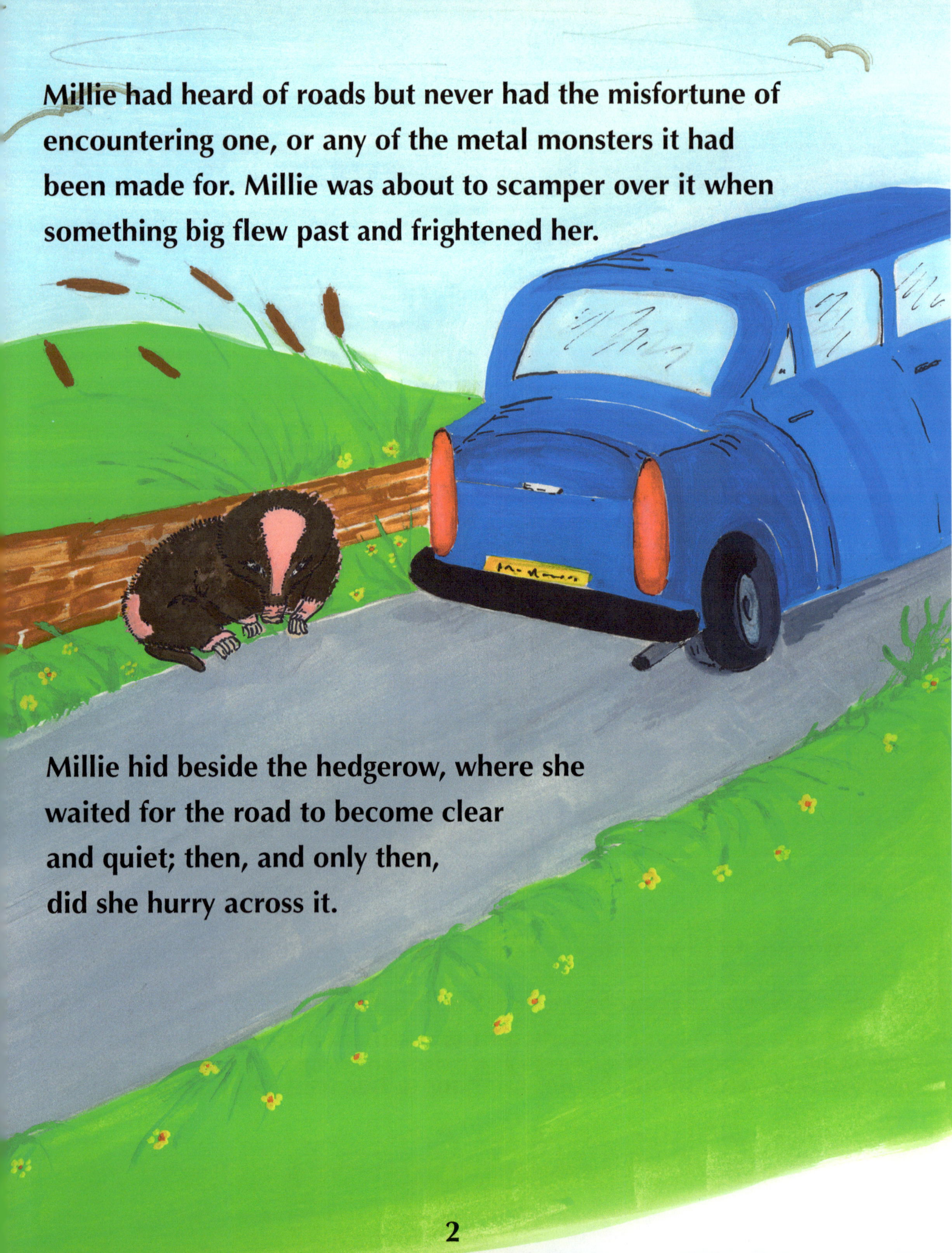

Millie had heard of roads but never had the misfortune of encountering one, or any of the metal monsters it had been made for. Millie was about to scamper over it when something big flew past and frightened her.

Millie hid beside the hedgerow, where she
waited for the road to become clear
and quiet; then, and only then,
did she hurry across it.

Millie had just begun to scamper along the
hedgerow, when a dark shadow fell upon her.
Rolling over, she saw Harry the Hawk.
The bird swooped downwards
and clutched Millie within its claws.

"Please don't eat me," Millie squealed. "I'm lost, and alone, and probably by now miles from home."

On hearing this, Harry hovered like a kite. "Why shouldn't I eat you, you're a juicy little snack. Just a silly mole fit only to dig a hole!"

"I may live underground but I'm not dozy or dull," pleaded Millie. "My hearing is sharp even in the dark. You may need me one day, just you wait and see!"

Millie's bravery amused Harry. "Go on," he laughed. "I'll be scouting about waiting to see what it is you can do for me."

Millie spotted a farmhouse and began scampering up towards it. She was some way there when she felt a paw push her to the ground. Millie wriggled upright and found Cleo the farm cat in her face.

"Please don't crush and crunch me, I got caught out by the concrete road..."

"Look at you; shiver and shake, a sprinkle of cheese and umm, in the oven you'd bake."

"I'm all skin and bone," Millie pleaded, "there's very little meat; I do however have excellent digging feet."

Cleo admired Millie's bravery, and released the young mole. "I'll be around to see what you can do for me."

Millie reached the farmhouse and glanced all around. Far in the distance she saw her mother, father, brother and sister. But a river at the bottom of the hill was separating them. Millie decided to swim across it and headed down the hill. She was halfway down when... whoosh... she was suddenly snapped up into the jaws of Fran Fox.

"Please don't eat me. I'm a bag of nerves, and if you hold me up I'll lose my family again."

Fran spat the mole out, and smiled at Millie.

"Why not? Beneath the morning sunlight you're quite an appetising sight, just a mere mole that lives in a dark hole."

"Please have a heart. Think yourself lucky you don't have to live in the dark. You may need my help one day."

Fran stepped back and frowned at Millie, "Brave, especially from someone in such a tight spot. I'll be watching you, to see what it is you can do for me!"

Millie made it to the river but was soon struggling to stay afloat. She pushed and pulled against the current, but was washed up onto some stones, where voices became crystal clear.

"For the next mile shoot everything in sight," one of them said.

With guns on their backs, men marched towards the farmhouse where Harry, Cleo and Fran were. Millie started to tear earth apart, digging furiously she tunnelled towards the farmhouse and animals.

8

Calling to the bird, the cat and the fox, she commanded
their attention. "Man is coming; bang boom bang,
he will shoot you for sure."

Sure enough the shot came and Harry flapped helplessly
to the floor.

"What shall we do?" Cleo and Fran asked Millie.

"Take Harry into the barn and wait for me there."

Quick as a flash, Millie dug and scratched until under the barn. Once there Millie made an even bigger hole that all of the animals got into.

Millie had just pulled leaves and straw over their heads when the hunters entered. Baffled by the disappearance of the hawk, they left in disappointment.

"There," Millie said. "I may be small but come rain, sun, or snow I am never slow." Using her teeth, she removed the bullet from Harry Hawk's wing.

"Now, if you don't mind, I'm going to find my family."

"How can we thank you?"
the three of them asked Millie.

"Be nice to all creatures great and small; we don't
have to be the menace that man is."

With that, Millie scampered away and finally found her family...

12

The End

www.ingramcontent.com/pod-product-compliance
Lightning Source LLC
Chambersburg PA
CBHW041614120626

46551CB00002B/441